On the LOOKOUT

Lives of Naturalists

Library of Congress Cataloging-in-Publication Data

Matthewson, Sarah.
  On the lookout : lives of naturalists / by Sarah Matthewson.
      p. cm. -- (Shockwave)
  Includes index.
  ISBN-10: 0-531-17772-6 (lib. bdg.)
  ISBN-13: 978-0-531-17772-3 (lib. bdg.)
  ISBN-10: 0-531-15499-8 (pbk.)
  ISBN-13: 978-0-531-15499-1 (pbk.)

  1. Naturalists--Biography--Juvenile literature. I. Title. II. Series.

  QH26.M29 2007
  508.092'2--dc22
  [B]

  2007018514

Published in 2008 by Children's Press, an imprint of Scholastic Inc.,
557 Broadway, New York, New York 10012
www.scholastic.com

08 09 10 11 12 13 14 15 16 17
10 9 8 7 6 5 4 3 2 1

Printed in China through Colorcraft Ltd., Hong Kong

Author: Sarah Matthewson
Educational Consultant: Ian Morrison
Editor: Karen Alexander
Designer: Emma Alsweiler
Photo Researchers: Sarah Matthewson and Karen Alexander

Photographs by: Big Stock Photo (p. 5; p. 22; p. 34); **©Bob Campbell/National Geographic Image Collection**
(pp. 26–27; Dian with Coco and Pucker, p. 29); **Courtesy of the Aldo Leopold Foundation Archives** (restoring the
Shack, p. 19); **Courtesy of the Lear/Carson Collection, Connecticut College** (#019 Rachel at Woods Hole Biological
Laboratory, 1929. Photo by Mary Frye, p. 20; #005 Rachel (about 5) reading to her dog, Candy. Carson Family
Photograph, p. 21); **Courtesy of Peter Unger** (p. 17); **©Estate of Gerald Durrell** (p. 24; Gerald Durrell as a boy, p. 25);
Getty Images (Earth Day, p. 9; Humboldt penguins, p. 11; p. 23); **Jennifer and Brian Lupton** (teenagers, pp. 32–33);
**John Muir Papers, Holt-Atherton Special Collections, University of the Pacific Library. Copyright 1984 Muir-Hanna
Trust** (John Muir, p. 14; glacier sketch, p. 15; Muir and friends, p. 17); **Julie Larsen Maher/©WCS–Wildlife Conservation
Society** (p. 31); **Library of Congress, Prints and Photographs Division** (Meriwether Lewis, John Muir, p. 8; William
Clark, John James Audubon, p. 9; p. 16); **Minden Pictures/Emerald City Images** (E.O. Wilson, p. 9; p. 30); **More
Images/FLPA** (p. 3; Darwin's finches, p. 13; p. 28); **Photolibrary** (p. 7; Charles Darwin, p. 13; tourist crowd, pp. 32–33);
StockCentral/TopFoto (Gerald Durrell, p. 9; p. 10); **Tranz/Corbis** (cover; Dian Fossey, p. 9; buzzard, p. 11; p. 12; giant
tortoise, p. 13; Mount Whitney, p. 15); **United States Fish and Wildlife Service** (Rachel Carson and Bob Hines, p. 21);
University of Wisconsin-Madison Archives (Aldo Leopold, p. 8; p. 18; journal, p. 19); **Yale Collection of American
Literature, Beinecke Rare Book and Manuscript Library** (coral reef, illustration by Bob Hines for Rachel Carson's
The Edge of the Sea, p. 21); **©Yann Arthus-Bertrand/Ardea** (Dian Fossey with guards and confiscated snares, p. 29)

The publisher would like to thank Peter Unger for the photo of KIPP Houston High School students at Yosemite National
Park on page 17.

All illustrations and other photographs © Weldon Owen Education Inc.

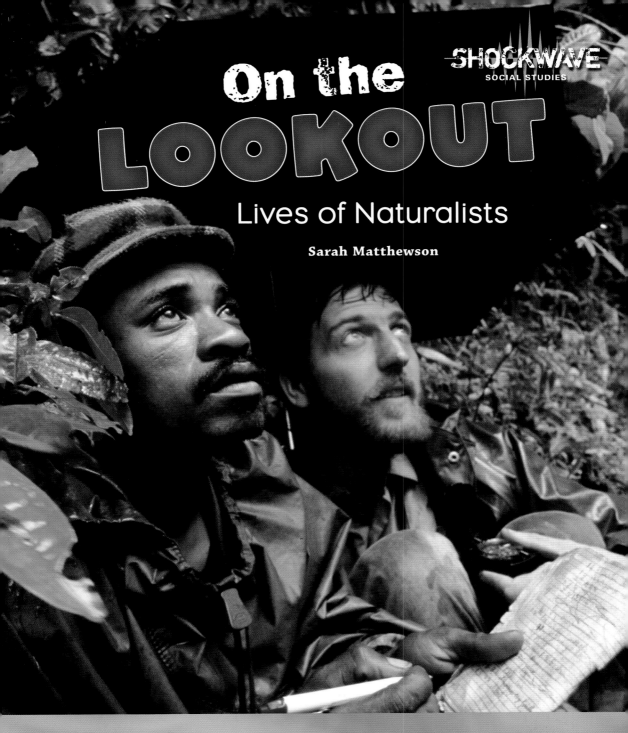

On the LOOKOUT

Lives of Naturalists

Sarah Matthewson

SHOCKWAVE
SOCIAL STUDIES

children's press®
An imprint of Scholastic Inc.
NEW YORK • TORONTO • LONDON • AUCKLAND • SYDNEY
MEXICO CITY • NEW DELHI • HONG KONG
DANBURY, CONNECTICUT

CHECK THESE OUT!

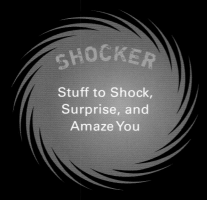

SHOCKER
Stuff to Shock, Surprise, and Amaze You

Quick Recaps and Notable Notes

Word Stunners and Other Oddities

The Heads-Up on Expert Reading

Links to More Information

CONTENTS

botanical (*boh TAN uh kuhl*) to do with the study of plants

conservationist (*kon sur VAY shuhn ist*) a person who works to protect plants, wildlife, and the environment

ecology (*ee KOL uh jee*) the study of the relationship between living things and their environment

expedition (*ek spuh DISH uhn*) a journey undertaken for a specific purpose

naturalist (*NACH ur uh list*) a person who studies nature

observation close examination of, and attention to, something

resistant able to survive the effects of a particular chemical

species (*SPEE sheez*) a group of plants or animals of the same kind

· ·

For additional vocabulary, see Glossary on page 34.

The *-ical* suffix on a word such as *botanical* usually makes the word an adjective. Other adjectives with this suffix include: *mechanical*, *comical*, *logical*, *tropical*, and *historical*.

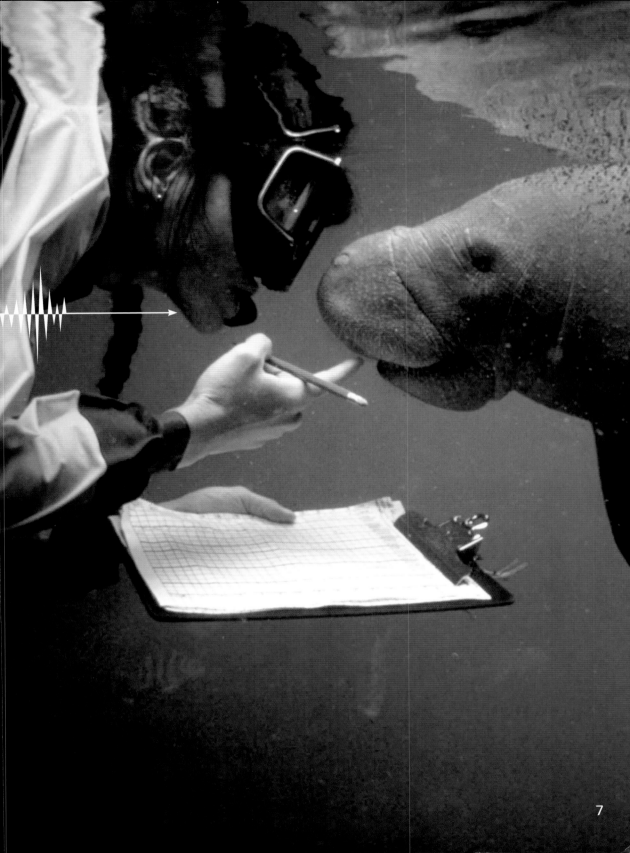

Carl Linnaeus
1707–1778

Meriwether Lewis
1744–1809

Alexander von Humboldt
1769–1859

Have you ever visited a national park, celebrated Earth Day, or read about global warming? If the answer is yes, thank a **naturalist**. A naturalist can be a scientist, a **conservationist**, or both. Today, conservationists and scientists who study nature need an understanding of **ecology**. In the past, however, many of the people who studied plants, animals, and the land did not understand the links between a **species** and its **habitat**. As for most other people, they believed that the wilderness and its resources were there for the taking! Pioneering conservationists battled to change that attitude.

Many of the naturalists in this book have been on the lookout in more ways than one. They have observed animal life. They have looked out for the environment by caring and campaigning for it. They have looked ahead, understanding that our actions create the world of the future. Most importantly, they haven't just looked out; they have spoken out.

John Muir
1838–1914

Aldo Leopold
1887–1948

Rachel Carson
1906–1964

William Clark
1770–1838

John James Audubon
1785–1851

Charles Darwin
1809–1882

People in many parts of the world observe Earth Day. They celebrate the beauty and **fragility** of the planet.

Gerald Durrell
1925–1995

Dian Fossey
1932–1985

Edward Wilson
1929–

THE GREAT ADVENTURE

The nineteenth century was an exciting time to be a naturalist. **Expeditions** of discovery set off from Europe to the most distant parts of the world. An amazing variety of natural life awaited naturalists. They returned from long, and often dangerous, journeys with a new kind of treasure – **specimens**. Their discoveries transformed Western knowledge of the natural world.

German naturalist Alexander von Humboldt studied nature in a big way. From plants to stars, little escaped his attention. Humboldt explored the Americas and Asia at the beginning of the nineteenth century. His **botanical** discoveries doubled the number of plant species known to western science. Humboldt had a great ambition: to publish a complete account of the physical world. His book *Cosmos* was a best seller – even though the index alone was 1,110 pages! Humboldt was a celebrity of his time. More places are named after him than almost any other scientist. They include 14 towns in the United States, numerous mountains, an ocean current, a **glacier**, and even a sea on the moon!

That's interesting! Humboldt was one of the names featured on the previous page. I wonder if each of the people on those pages will be featured somewhere in the book. I'll keep a "lookout" for them!

Humboldt and his team in the Andes, in South America

Alexander von Humboldt

In the past, naturalists didn't study animals in their natural habitats. They killed them to study them.

These are Humboldt, or Peruvian, penguins. There is also a giant squid named after Humboldt.

Born in Haiti, artist and naturalist John James Audubon set out in the 1820s to paint as many of the bird species of North America as possible. Audubon killed the birds, then arranged them in a realistic pose to paint them! On one occasion Audubon said, "I shot some rare birds. I believe I would have shot 100 … had not a mistake taken place in the loading of my gun."

Naturalist Notes

In 1758, the Swedish naturalist Carl Linnaeus published a universal **classification** system for naming and grouping plants and animals. Linnaeus sent his students to collect specimens from Africa, Asia, and the Americas. By the 1800s, expeditions of discovery nearly always included a naturalist.

Californian buzzard painted by Audubon

> "Nothing can be more improving to a young naturalist than a journey in distant countries." – Charles Darwin

In 1804, two American explorers, Meriwether Lewis and William Clark, set out on an expedition along the Missouri River. They hoped to find a navigable water route all the way west to the Pacific Ocean. President Jefferson thought they might also find woolly mammoths. They didn't find either. However, they did find 178 plants and 123 animals that had never before been recorded, including the western red cedar, the coyote, the plains gray wolf, and the grizzly bear – although they had already been warned by Native Americans about these large and dangerous animals. The Clark's crow and the Lewis's woodpecker are named after the explorers.

SHOCKER

Early naturalists often risked death in the pursuit of science. Scottish botanist George Forrest reported being hunted like a wild beast by tribesmen in western China. He escaped, but he lost his collection of 2,000 plant and 80 seed specimens.

Early Naturalists

- Humboldt – wrote about new species
- Audubon – painted rare birds
- Linnaeus – created classification system
- Darwin – formed theory of evolution
- Lewis and Clark – found new plants and animals

Sacagawea (*sah kah guh WEE uh*) was a Shoshone Native American. She and her French husband were hired by Lewis and Clark as interpreters. She was the only woman to complete the round trip.

In 1831, a young British naturalist named Charles Darwin set sail on a round-the-world survey voyage. He returned with a **revolutionary** idea about life on the earth. It took him almost 20 years to gather the evidence and the courage to publish his theory. As Darwin had feared, his book *The Origin of Species* caused an uproar. In his book, Darwin put forward his theory of **evolution**. It was an enormously controversial idea. In fact, people still argue about it today.

For the most part, these early naturalists looked at all of nature – both animals and plants. Gradually, however, the study of natural history led into more **specialized** areas. For example, biology was divided into separate subjects, such as **zoology** and botany. Many naturalists began to specialize in one field.

Charles Darwin

Darwin spent five years sailing around the world. He landed at many places, where he observed the plants and animals, taking notes and collecting specimens. His **observations** of the huge tortoises at the Galápagos Islands contributed to his theory of evolution.

ON

THE ORIGIN OF SPECIES

BY MEANS OF NATURAL SELECTION,

OR THE

PRESERVATION OF FAVOURED RACES IN THE STRUGGLE FOR LIFE.

By CHARLES DARWIN, M.A.,

FELLOW OF THE ROYAL, GEOLOGICAL, LINNÆAN, ETC., SOCIETIES;
AUTHOR OF 'JOURNAL OF RESEARCHES DURING H. M. S. BEAGLE'S VOYAGE
ROUND THE WORLD.'

Darwin brought back 13 species of finch from the Galápagos Islands. The birds had similar bodies, but very different beaks. Darwin concluded that the finches had evolved over time to feed on different foods. Here are four of the birds, on the title page of his book.

JOHN MUIR
From John O'Mountains to Ice Chief

In 1860, a scruffy, twenty-two-year-old left the family farm in Wisconsin in search of his life's work. John Muir was a genius at mechanical invention, but his passion was for nature. Muir's schooling had ended when the family left Scotland for the United States. From the age of eleven, he worked 17-hour days, helping to farm the land. The work was difficult, and Muir's father treated him harshly. When he was older, Muir realized that all these experiences had been good training for wilderness survival!

In 1868, Muir discovered the place that suited his vision of the perfect wilderness – Yosemite (*Yo SEH mih tee*) Valley, in California. What forces had created such an awe-inspiring landscape? On a quest to find out, Muir became a detective as well as a mountaineer. He filled endless notebooks with observations and drawings, earning the nickname "John O'Mountains." Muir's conclusion that ancient glaciers had carved out the valley was doubted by the state **geologist**, but in 1871 Muir found proof – a surviving glacier.

A fascination with the power of ice lured Muir to Alaska in 1879. The Tlingit people who accompanied him on his expedition were amazed by the way he coped with storms and high cliffs of ice. They gave him a new nickname, "the ice chief."

Muir didn't care about appearances or money. He wrote in his journal, "I could have been a millionaire, but I chose to become a tramp."

Muir thrived on danger. He once climbed a tree so that he could sway with it in a strong gale. His other adventures included an unexpected ride on the crest of an avalanche!

Mount Whitney

When Muir was caught outdoors overnight below the icy summit of Mount Whitney, he danced all night to stay warm and keep himself from being frozen.

Naturalist Notes

When he was twenty-nine, Muir had a job in a woodworking factory. One night, a tool hit him in the eye. For a month he lay in a darkened room, fearing he would never again see his beloved trees. When he got his sight back, he resolved to dedicate his life to the wilderness!

Muir sketched himself climbing a glacier in the Sierra Nevadas.

15

John Muir hated cities and crowds. He was happiest living alone in the wilderness. However, the wish to preserve Yosemite Valley as a wilderness changed Muir from a wanderer to a fighter for conservation. He campaigned tirelessly for the valley's preservation, writing nine books, more than 400 articles, and thousands of letters.

In 1903, when Muir was about to leave on a trip to Europe, a message came from President Theodore Roosevelt. Muir's articles about Yosemite Valley had impressed the president. He wanted to see the valley for himself. The men spent four days trekking in the wilderness without tents. They used branches for bedding. Muir showed Roosevelt the immense ancient sequoias that were more precious to him than any cathedral. Over the campfire, Muir described how the "tree killers," as he called lumbermen, were destroying the forest while flocks of "hoofed locusts" (sheep) ate their way through the valley's meadows.

Earlier campaigning by Muir had resulted in the establishment of Yosemite National Park in 1890. In 1906, Yosemite Valley was added to the national park. John Muir's most enduring legacy is this land that he fought for.

"When we try to pick out anything by itself, we find it hitched to everything else in the universe." – John Muir

John Muir (right) and President Roosevelt stand at Glacier Point, above Yosemite Valley. The Yosemite trip greatly influenced Roosevelt, who became known as "the conservation president." In all, he set aside 230 million acres as protected land.

Muir and friends in Sequoia National Park

Naturalist Notes

In Muir's time, most people saw land as a resource to be used. Muir called it "the gobble, gobble economy." Sequoia trees – the largest living things on the earth – were being chopped down without any thought. Muir hoped that, if people could see the wilderness as he did, they wouldn't be in such a rush to destroy it. Sequoias once grew over most of the northern hemisphere. Now they grow only on the western slopes of the Sierra Nevada mountains.

I guess these pages are still about John Muir. Reading the clues is important, and there are lots of them: there is no main heading; the page on the right has "John Muir continued" at the top; and the background color is the same as the previous pages.

Muir was one of the founders of the Sierra Club, which plays an important role both in conservation and in educating people about the wilderness. Some of these students from Houston, Texas, had never seen snow before their trip to Yosemite National Park.

ALDO LEOPOLD
Reading the Land

Even as a child growing up in Iowa, Aldo Leopold loved observing nature. He was often found roaming the land, binoculars and notebook in hand. His classmates called him "the naturalist."

Fresh out of Yale Forestry School in 1909, Leopold's first job took him to Arizona's Apache National Forest as a forest ranger. Leopold loved the wild southwest. He dressed like a cowboy and was, as he later described it, "full of **trigger itch**." He loved to hunt wolves and bears. However, he soon made a surprising discovery. The loss of these **predators** was not healthy for the mountains. Overgrazing by sheep and deer was disastrous for the land. Leopold looked to the wilderness for lessons on how to restore balance to damaged environments. He persuaded the Forest Service to create the nation's first Wilderness Area, at Gila in New Mexico.

In 1933, Leopold became a professor of game management at the University of Wisconsin-Madison. He took his students outdoors and asked them questions such as: Why is this field abandoned? When was the last hard winter? To answer questions like these, Leopold told his students that they must read not books but the landscape itself. Leopold rolled up his shirtsleeves and "read" the landscape at his own Wisconsin farm. This weedy property gave him a perfect opportunity to practice his theories about restoring land. Leopold's extraordinary powers of observation made him a pioneer in ecology, conservation, and wildlife management.

Leopold never forgot the fierce green light in the eyes of a dying wolf that he had shot. Ranchers and forest rangers saw wolves, grizzlies, and pumas as pests to be destroyed. But without predators, the deer population increased rapidly. The population then fell drastically because there was not enough food. Today, ecologists understand the vital role of predators. Many of these important animals, from wolves to sharks, are now protected.

Leopold as a forest ranger

> "The outstanding scientific discovery of the twentieth century is not television or radio, but rather the complexity of the land organism." – Aldo Leopold

SHOCKER

In 1913, Leopold got very ill after sleeping on a wet bedroll in a storm. He took 18 months to recover. After that, he was too weak to continue to work as a forest ranger.

Leopold deliberately selected his Wisconsin farm, "the shack," because it was run down. The only building, the chicken coop, was full of chicken and cow manure. Leopold and his family renovated it so that they could stay in it. One daughter said, "What could be more of a challenge for a bunch of teenagers?"

Naturalist Notes

In his book *A Sand County Almanac*, Leopold said: "We abuse land because we regard it as a commodity belonging to us. When we see land as a community to which we belong, we may begin to use it with love and respect." In 1935, Leopold helped to found the Wilderness Society, which works to save, protect, and restore America's wilderness areas.

Aldo Leopold died of a heart attack in 1948 while helping to fight a fire that was threatening his beloved pine trees. His singed journal was found in his pocket.

RACHEL CARSON
In Love With the Sea

As a child, Rachel Carson dreamed of being a writer. She also dreamed of the ocean, which lay hundreds of miles from her family's farm in Springdale, Pennsylvania. Rachel was short, slight, and extremely shy. Only those closest to her knew of her love of fun and her determination. Carson finally had her first encounter with the ocean when she attended a summer school at the Marine Biological Laboratory at Woods Hole, Massachusetts. She fell in love with the sea, and with its inhabitants.

Carson juggled part-time jobs to fund her master's degree in zoology. When her father died in 1935, she needed to get a job to support her family. Further study was impossible. Finding work during the **Great Depression** wasn't easy for anyone, let alone a woman who wanted to be a marine biologist. Carson leapt at the offer of a job preparing radio scripts on marine life for the Bureau of Fisheries. The work combined her passions: writing and marine biology. A year later, after getting the top score in a civil service examination, Carson was offered a job as a biologist with the bureau.

From the time Carson first saw the ocean, it was her passion. She wrote three books about it: *Under the Sea Wind* (1941), *The Sea Around Us* (1951), and *The Edge of the Sea* (1955). *The Sea Around Us* was on the best-seller list for 81 weeks.

Carson loved tide-pooling – collecting and examining specimens from rock pools at low tide. Sometimes she risked **hypothermia** from standing for hours in cold water. Once, she became so numb that she had to be carried ashore by Bob Hines, her illustrator (shown here tide-pooling with Carson).

Sketch by Bob Hines for *The Edge of the Sea*

Carson always loved writing. She was only ten when she published her first story, which appeared in a magazine for young writers.

From Silent Spring to Noisy Summer

Carson gradually became very concerned about the effect of poisons on the ecology of the ocean and also of the land. In 1962, she published *Silent Spring*, a book about the dangers of **pesticide** use. Readers were gripped by the book's opening vision: life in a vibrant rural town changes suddenly after an unidentified white powder falls from the sky. The dawn chorus of birdsong is replaced by a strange silence. *Silent Spring* started a national debate about the impact on the ecology of chemicals, especially **DDT**. A journalist joked that "*Silent Spring* was followed by a noisy summer." The uproar reached all the way to the White House. President Kennedy appointed a committee to examine the use of pesticides.

Opening a hearing on environmental hazards in June 1963, Senator Ribicoff said: "Miss Carson ... you are the lady who started all this." Carson's book helped people to understand the need to protect the environment. It showed the harm that pesticides could do to both ecology and human health. Carson pointed out that the long-term effects of pesticides were still unknown. She did not argue that pesticides should be banned. She simply wanted caution and strict testing standards. Within months of the book's publication, legislation restricting the use of chemicals had been introduced across the United States. DDT was banned in the U.S. in 1972.

Rachel Carson is seen by many people as the mother of the environmental movement. In the years after the publication of *Silent Spring*, the environmental movement took off. The Environmental Protection Agency was set up in 1970. Environmentalists today continue to honor Rachel Carson as the person "who started all this."

In *Silent Spring*, Carson said that aerial spraying can make problems worse. It can kill both the pests and their natural predators. Some pests become **resistant** to the chemicals. Also, without the predators, the pest populations can increase quickly.

"I have tried to say that all the life of the planet is interrelated, that each species has its own ties to others, and that all are related to earth." – Rachel Carson

Carson believed it was important to share children's sense of wonder at the natural world.

Silent Spring

- published in 1962
- highlighted pesticide problems
- started national debate
- brought about law changes
- led to banning of DDT

SHOCKER

The manufacture of pesticides is a multimillion-dollar industry. The National Agricultural Chemicals Association spent a quarter of a million dollars on its campaign to disprove Carson's research and prevent her from publishing her book.

Naturalist Notes

Public recognition for Rachel Carson has included:

- Ecology Hall of Fame
- National Women's Hall of Fame
- *TIME* magazine: One of the 100 most important people of the twentieth century
- New York University School of Journalism: *Silent Spring* – one of the top 100 works of journalism in the U.S. in the twentieth century
- Presidential Medal of Freedom

Naturalist Peter Matthiessen said about Rachel Carson: "Before there was an environmental movement, there was one brave woman and her very brave book."

GERALD DURRELL
From Collecting to Conservation

Even as a very young child, Gerald Durrell was obsessed with animals. The first word his mother remembered him saying was *zoo*. As a boy, he wasn't interested in sports or school or playing with other children. Instead he spent hours tracking the wildlife on Corfu, the Greek island his family moved to when he was ten. By then, he had two ambitions – to collect animals for zoos and to open a zoo of his own.

In his early twenties, Durrell made headlines when he returned from a trip to West Africa with hundreds of unusual creatures, such as hairy frogs and flying squirrels. He spent the next ten years visiting remote countries. To Durrell's amazement, the books he wrote about his adventures became best-sellers. The books were wildly funny, but Durrell had a serious mission – to save rare animals from extinction.

In 1959, Durrell finally realized his dream when he opened his own zoo on the island of Jersey, in the Channel Islands, near Britain. His main purpose for the zoo – the breeding of endangered species – was considered revolutionary then. Now, thanks to Durrell and others like him, similar programs are run in zoos all around the world.

Durrell focused on saving the smaller endangered animals, such as this silky anteater from Panama.

Statues of dodos stand at the entrance to Durrell zoo. Durrell chose the dodo as the symbol for the zoo. He wanted to prevent other animals sharing the fate of the dodo, which was hunted to extinction. Children up to age sixteen can join the zoo's Dodo Club. A number of them have gone on to careers as naturalists.

Learn more at: www.durrellwildlife.org.

Zoo is short for *zoological garden*. Often, short forms of words become acceptable because they are convenient. Some include: *phone* (telephone); *TV* (television); *vet* (veterinarian).

Naturalist Notes

Durrell narrowly survived a potentially fatal snake bite while he was in West Africa. However, that didn't end his interest in the reptiles. When he heard about an old drainage pit full of vipers, he found it irresistible! He got to the pit at night, and was lowered into it by rope. At one point, his lamp went out. Then he lost a shoe. But, using a forked stick, he managed to bag 12 Gaboon vipers, one of the deadliest species of central Africa.

On Corfu, Durrell was taught at home by private teachers. They found that the only subject he was interested in was natural history.

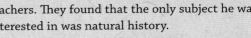

DIAN FOSSEY
Life and Death With Mountain Gorillas

In 1963, a tall, gangly American tourist visited an archaeological site in Tanzania, where she met a famous **paleontologist**, Dr. Louis Leakey. She later climbed the 10,000-foot-high Virunga mountains, where she saw mountain gorillas for the first time. These two encounters shaped Dian Fossey's future.

Three years later, Leakey chose Fossey to conduct a long-term study of the Virunga mountain gorillas. She did not have any zoological training, and was prone to respiratory illnesses. What she did have was determination and a passion to observe gorillas closely in their own habitat.

For her first two years, Fossey trailed the gorillas, observing nine different groups. Over time, the gorillas became accustomed to her presence. She was gradually able to approach closer and closer to their groups as they browsed for food. Then, one day, something astonishing happened. A bold gorilla infant that she had named Peanuts approached her, reached out, and touched her outstretched hand. She was an honorary gorilla – she had been accepted into the clan!

Dian Fossey was the first gorilla researcher to make friends with the animals.

One mistake Fossey made at the beginning of her study was to imitate gorilla chest-pounding. This is a challenge to a gorilla. Luckily, when a young male charged, Fossey remembered what to do – crouch, lower your eyes, and stay very still!

Dian Fossey at work in her hut

Naturalist Notes

Fossey set up her research center in a remote part of Rwanda. She called the center Karisoke after two nearby mountains – Karisimbi and Visoke. It rains heavily at Karisoke for part of every day. The land is steep and the temperatures are chilly. You need a machete to cut a path through the dense vegetation. The nearest village is two hours' trek away. The sociable Fossey sometimes got "the astronaut blues." She would get the shakes and be unable to stop crying. Some of her student helpers couldn't cope with the isolation and the climate. One student left after three days.

To get close to the gorillas, Fossey had to become one – at least in their eyes. She learned gorilla body language – scratching, grooming, and belching.

27

Fossey wrote about how gorillas relate to one another and the way they live. But the gorillas were far more than research subjects to her. She grew to know and care passionately about them as individuals. One **silverback**, Digit, was a special favorite. She watched him grow from a playful infant into the protector of his family group. Digit's slaughter by **poachers** in January 1978 devastated Fossey. Her anger quickly turned to action. She stepped up her tactics against poachers, destroying their traps, burning their camps, and stealing their weapons.

The tough conditions at Karisoke took a terrible toll on Fossey. The climate was bad for her health. By the early 1980s, she was too frail to keep up her regular visits to the gorilla groups in the jungle. However, she hated to be away from Karisoke. The fight to protect the gorillas was her life. Now she was concerned about a possible new threat to the gorillas and their habitat – the number of tourists who wanted to see these rare animals.

Fossey was murdered at Karisoke on December 27, 1985. Her murderer has never been caught. She was probably killed by poachers, who resented her actions against them. Fossey was buried close to her precious Digit. Today her mission to safeguard the survival of mountain gorillas is continued by the Dian Fossey Gorilla Fund.

Dian Fossey is buried in her gorilla cemetery alongside the graves of gorillas who were killed by poachers.

Dian Fossey's grave

Fossey picked up gorilla body language from her observations, but two orphaned baby gorillas taught her what gorilla sounds mean. She learned that gorillas make more than 20 different sounds, each with its own meaning. Coco and Pucker had been captured for sale to zoos but had become ill. Fossey was allowed to take them to nurse them back to health. She devoted herself to their recovery, turning her hut into a gorilla nursery, complete with jungle vegetation.

SHOCKER

One of the students at Karisoke researched gorilla parasites and had the very smelly job of dissecting gorilla droppings to count the tapeworms. Fossey nicknamed him "worm boy."

Parasite refers to a plant or an animal that lives and feeds on another plant or animal. The word is related to the Greek word *parasitos* – a person who eats at the table of another!

Naturalist Notes

Fossey was one of three women selected by Louis Leakey to study the great apes. Leakey believed that women have greater persistence than men, and therefore make better **primatologists**. Years of continuous and patient observation are necessary to document primate behavior fully. Leakey chose well. Jane Goodall spent 45 years learning about chimpanzees. Biruté Galdikas has been working with orangutans since 1971. Dian Fossey devoted 18 years to researching mountain gorillas.

Fossey and her guards tried to protect the gorillas by collecting the snares used by poachers. Fighting poachers became more important to Fossey than information gathering. She called her policy "active conservation." How could she stand by doing research on the animals while letting their populations plummet through inaction?

29

LOOKING OUT TODAY

▶ Edward O. Wilson

As a young boy, Edward Wilson dreamed of discovering a giant sea monster. However, his life took a very different turn. Wilson's sight was damaged in a fishing accident. Afterwards, it was easier for him to look at small animals than large ones. He became famous for his research on ant behavior. However, Wilson loves thinking big. His biggest idea yet is the *Encyclopedia of Life*. The encyclopedia will be an online database of all the existing knowledge about plant and animal species. Each species will have its own Web page. The project will involve not simply scientific institutions and researchers, but biology enthusiasts everywhere.

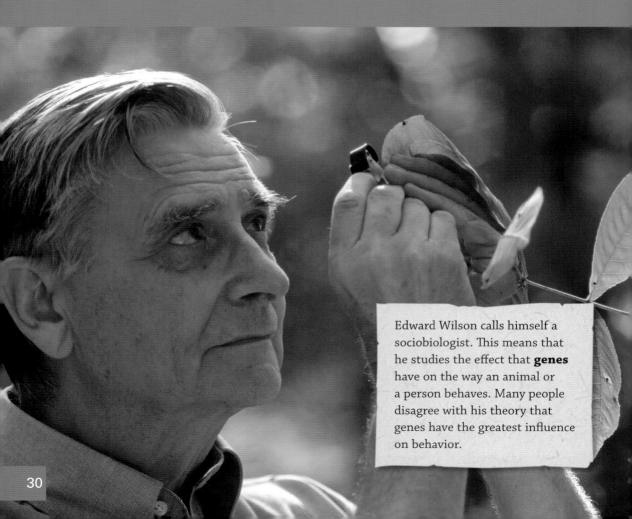

Edward Wilson calls himself a sociobiologist. This means that he studies the effect that **genes** have on the way an animal or a person behaves. Many people disagree with his theory that genes have the greatest influence on behavior.

Endless discoveries remain to be made about the natural world, and it needs our protection more than ever! Naturalists need not be scientists. Thousands of people around the world are involved in studying nature, in preserving it, and in sharing their love of it with others.

Characteristics of Naturalists

determination

vision

courage

observation skills

perseverance

passion

Mananjo Jonahson

It's probably safe to get this close to a shark jaw only when it's a skeleton! The jawbone has given marine biologist Mananjo Jonahson valuable clues about the shark's health and diet. However, Jonahson prefers sharks alive. She works for the Wildlife Conservation Society, developing ways to protect the sharks around Madagascar. She carries out most of her shark studies in the waters off the island. The rapid decline in the number of sharks is due to overfishing. Sharks, along with other large marine species, such as dugongs and dolphins, are vital to Madagascar's marine ecosystem. Jonahson wants people to realize how important sharks are to the ecology of the ocean, and to stop regarding them as something to be feared and destroyed.

...ught to save Yosemite from development so that people could enjoy its unspoiled beauty. Today, more than three million tourists visit the park every year. Within the park boundaries there are shops, hotels, a golf course, an ice-skating rink, and massive parking lots. The park's popularity threatens the very wilderness people come to marvel at. Many national parks and wilderness areas face the same problem.

WHAT DO YOU THINK?

Do you think that protecting nature is more important than letting people visit wilderness areas and animals in their natural habitat?

PRO

Thinking that people always come first has gotten our environment into a mess. People are often too greedy! There's a difference between wanting and needing. Many species are becoming endangered or are extinct because of humans. We need to protect wild places and their animals, not exploit them.

People who work to protect endangered animals worry that their campaigning may make the animals too popular. For example, many tourists travel to see the 700 or so remaining mountain gorillas. There is concern that the animals will become stressed. Their habitat may be disturbed, disrupting their lives. Also, increased familiarity with humans may make the gorillas more vulnerable to poachers.

CON

Naturalists won't succeed in protecting the natural environment unless they have people's support. People would resent being told they could not visit one of their own national parks. Also, many tourists go a long way to see animals in the wild. It may be the only chance they will ever have to see those animals.

GLOSSARY

classification (*klass uh fuh KAY shuhn*) the division of things, such as animals and plants, into groups of similar things

DDT a chemical used to kill insects

evolution (*ev uh LOO shuhn*) the gradual changes that occur in living things over thousands of years

fragility (*frah JIL it ee*) the condition of being easily damaged

gene part of the DNA in a cell that controls one aspect of the way a living thing looks or how it behaves

geologist (*jee OL uh jist*) a scientist who studies the rocks, soil, and minerals of Earth

glacier (*GLAY shur*) a large mass of slow-moving ice

Great Depression the collapse of the world economy in the 1930s

habitat the area where a plant or an animal lives naturally

hypothermia (*hye poh THUR mee uh*) a major lowering of the body temperature that can cause death

paleontologist (*pale ee uhn TOL uh jist*) a person who studies fossils and early forms of life

pesticide a chemical that kills pests, especially insects

poacher a person who takes or kills an animal without permission

predator an animal that hunts other animals for food

primatologist (*prye muh TOL uh jist*) a scientist who studies primates, such as gorillas

revolutionary (*rev uh LOO shuhn air ee*) completely new and different

silverback an adult male gorilla with silvery gray hair on its back

specialized (*SPESH uh lized*) focused on just one kind of work

specimen (*SPESS uh muhn*) a sample of something, used to represent the whole species

Silverback

trigger itch the tendency to shoot at something without thinking

zoology (*zoh OL uh jee*) the science that studies animal life

FIND OUT MORE

BOOKS

Jackson, Donna M. *The Wildlife Detectives: How Forensic Scientists Fight Crimes Against Nature*. Houghton Mifflin, 2000.

Levine, Ellen. *Up Close: Rachel Carson*. Viking, 2007.

Naden, Corinne J. and Blue, Rose. *Dian Fossey: At Home with the Giant Gorillas*. Millbrook Press, 2002.

Swinburne, Stephen R. *The Woods Scientist*. Houghton Mifflin, 2002.

Topp, Patricia. *Call Him Father Nature: The Story of John Muir*. Blue Dolphin Publishing, 2001.

Yannuzzi, Della. *Aldo Leopold: Protector of the Wild*. Millbrook Press, 2002.

WEB SITES

Go to the Web sites below to learn more about wildlife and conservation.

www.wildlife-international.org/index.html

www.ecotopia.org/ehof/muir/bio.html

www.gorillafund.org/dian_fossey

http://pbskids.org/zoom/activities/action/way04.html

INDEX

ABOUT THE AUTHOR

Sarah Matthewson once dreamed of becoming a naturalist, so she found it inspiring to research and write about the achievements of naturalists. Sarah belongs to a number of conservation organizations in New Zealand, where she lives. Whenever possible, she loves escaping city life to go hiking in wilderness areas and national parks. Sarah hopes that reading about the individuals profiled in this book will inspire young people to explore the natural environment and get involved in conservation.